Stay Close to Mama

by Toni Buzzeo

Illustrated by Mike Wohnoutka

DISNEY • HYPERION

LOS ANGELES NEW YORK

First Edition, March 2012
10 9 8 7 6 5 4
H106-9333-5-14349
Printed in Malaysia
Designed by Michelle Gengaro-Kokmen
Reinforced binding

Library of Congress Cataloging-in-Publication Data

Buzzeo, Toni.
Stay close to mama / Toni Buzzeo ; illustrations by Mike Wohnoutka.—1st ed.
p. cm.
Summary: A curious baby giraffe keeps wandering away from his mother
to explore the interesting sights and smells that surround them.
Includes a note on giraffes.
ISBN 978-1-4231-3482-4 (hardcover)
[1. Giraffe—Fiction. 2. Animals—Infancy—Fiction. 3. Mother and child—Fiction.]
I. Wohnoutka, Mike, ill. II. Title.
PZ7.B9832St 2012
[E]—dc23
2011011110

Visit www.DisneyBooks.com

To Janie, who taught me, who believed with me,
and who never gave up hope, with a world of love and gratitude
—T.B.

To Linda and Carol, two wonderful mamas
—M.W.

Beneath the bright yellow sun,
in the high dry grass,
Twiga peeks from under
his tall, tall mama.

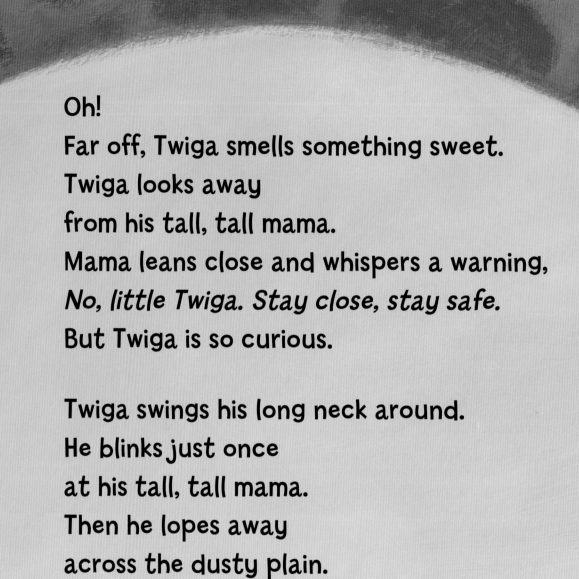

Oh!
Far off, Twiga smells something sweet.
Twiga looks away
from his tall, tall mama.
Mama leans close and whispers a warning,
No, little Twiga. Stay close, stay safe.
But Twiga is so curious.

Twiga swings his long neck around.
He blinks just once
at his tall, tall mama.
Then he lopes away
across the dusty plain.

Twiga brushes past
a termite mound,
where a hyena rests in the shade.

Mama's legs swish
in the tall brown grass.

Oh!

Over there, Twiga hears something sing.

No, little Twiga. Stay close, stay safe.

But Twiga is so curious.

Twiga trots off
across shimmering sand
right past his tall, tall mama.

Dust swirls up
from Twiga's hard hooves.
His nostrils close tight
as he lopes downhill.

Oh!
Coming near, Twiga hears the music.
No, little Twiga. Stay close, stay safe.
But Twiga is so curious.

Twiga's hooves clatter
as the thorny tree whistles
across from his tall, tall mama.

OUCH!
Stinging ants stream
from the whistling thorns.
Twiga shakes, Twiga shivers, Twiga runs.

Oh!
Down below, Twiga spots a sparkle.
No, little Twiga. Stay close, stay safe.
But Twiga is so curious.

Twiga gallops down
the long brown slope
far from his tall, tall mama.

Ground grows muddy
as Twiga draws nearer.
Twiga sees the sunlight
shining up at him.

Oh!
Just ahead, Twiga sees something glitter.
No, little Twiga. Stay close, stay safe.
But Twiga is so curious.
Twiga steps along
the squishy, slippery shore
far from his tall, tall mama.

He s t r e t c h e s his neck
and r e a c h e s his tongue
and then . . .

KA-SPLOSH!

Oh no!

Wet all around.

Twiga splashes, Twiga kicks,

Twiga stands.

Two eyes stare above snapping jaws.
Twiga swings his head around,
from side to side.
He searches for his tall, tall mama.

Suddenly, on the wind,
that delicious smell
tickles Twiga's twitchy nose again.
And Twiga is still curious.

Oh!
Up ahead, a sausage tree towers.
No, little Twiga! Stay close! Stay safe!
But Twiga is so curious.

Twiga takes a slipping step
like a hippo walking.
Twiga takes a sliding step
toward the tasty smell.

At last!
He grabs sweet fruit
from the towering tree,
then gallops away
from the danger lurking.

Oh!
Right here, Mama is waiting.
She licks his head
and nuzzles him close.
My little Twiga!
Now you're here and safe.
Twiga snuggles up against
her tall, warm side.
He's here to stay.

Then he looks away
from his tall, tall mama
at the wide, shining world.

And Twiga is so curious.

Author's Note

In Swahili, *twiga* is the word for giraffe. Giraffes are very curious creatures. However, they rarely allow humans within one hundred feet of them. In addition, they are one of the few land mammals that cannot swim. They have a strong dislike of water, never go into the water to bathe, and even hide their heads among the dense acacia leaves to keep the rain off their faces. In addition to acacia leaves, giraffes enjoy the sweet fruit of the sausage tree (also called the kigelia tree), with its strange batlike odor.